THE GHOST SHIP

3-D PUZZLE STORYBOOK

Written by Fiona Conboy
Illustrated by John Lennard

INSTRUCTIONS

- Read the directions at the top of each page.
- Solve the puzzles in the correct order.
  They are numbered 1 to 23.
- The answer to each puzzle is a letter.
  Write down your answers as you go.
- At the end of the book, your answers will
  spell out the location of the treasure.
- The answers are listed at the back of the book.

Good luck!

Cartwheel
B·O·O·K·S ®

SCHOLASTIC INC.

New York Toronto London Auckland Sydney

On an empty beach, you come across an old bottle with a scroll of paper inside. At the top is a series of symbols, and at the bottom is a message which reads:

"Find the remains of the old ship, the Specter. Climb aboard if you dare. As you explore the ship, solve each puzzle—your answers will provide the key to this mysterious message."

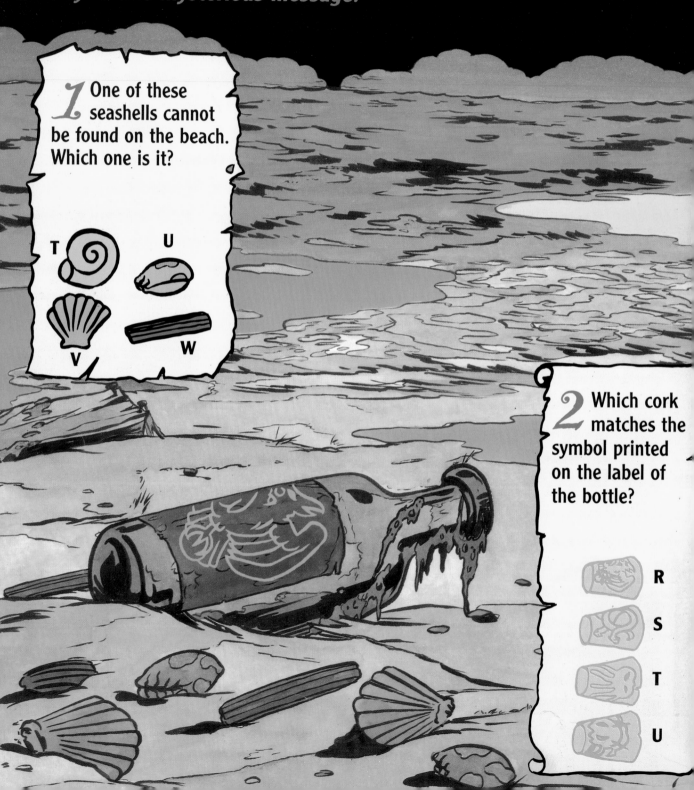

1 One of these seashells cannot be found on the beach. Which one is it?

T
U
V
W

2 Which cork matches the symbol printed on the label of the bottle?

R
S
T
U

Ahead of you lies the *Specter*. The ship creaks loudly as it sways in the wind. You climb bravely on board in your search for clues!

3 There are several loose ropes at your feet. Which one leads to the ship?

F   E   G

The main deck is empty.
You begin to explore this ghost ship.

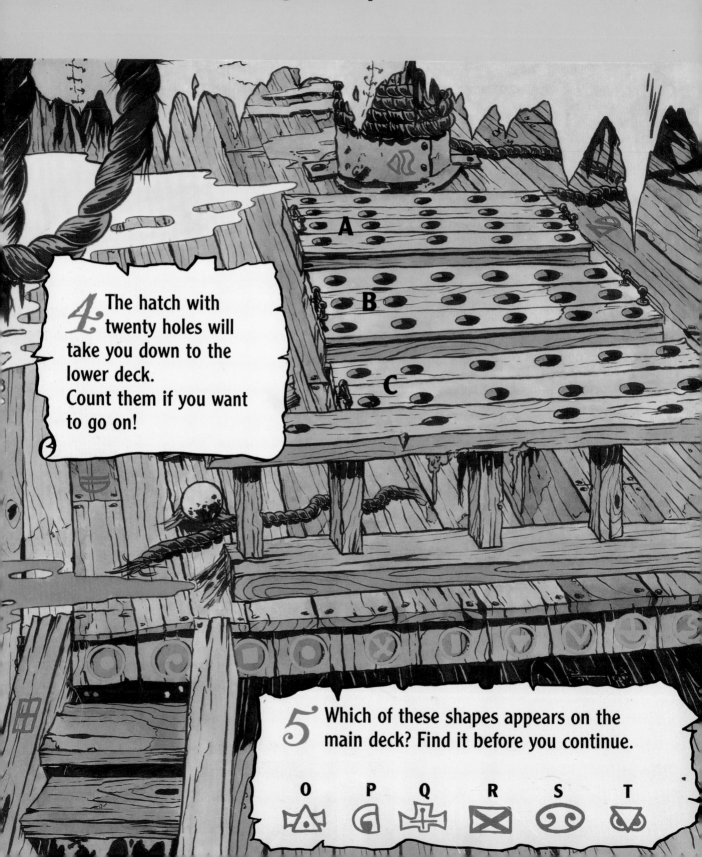

A

B

C

4 The hatch with twenty holes will take you down to the lower deck. Count them if you want to go on!

5 Which of these shapes appears on the main deck? Find it before you continue.

O   P   Q   R   S   T

At the other end of the deck, you see the entrance to the wheel house. Solve the next puzzle and you can move on.

As you enter the wheel house, the wheel appears to be moving! Perhaps you are not alone.

7 How many nails can you count on the hatch?

Q
15

R
18

S
20

You feel sure someone else is on board the ship—but you can't see who it is. You hurry toward the next cabin.

8 There is a piece missing from the wheel. Can you find it?

B C D E

9 Can you find this shape in the picture?

On entering the captain's cabin—S M A S H !—a pane of glass from the window shatters at your feet. Was it the wind outside, or is someone trying to stop you from finding the treasure?

10 Only one entrance will lead you through the maze.

O

N

P

EXIT HERE

As you tread carefully around the broken glass on the table you see the sparkling jeweled goblet that must have belonged to the captain. You also spot the remains of the last meal he had!

11 Can you find the missing piece of glass from the shattered pane?

Q R S T U

12 Which one of these jewels does not appear on the captain's cup?

F
G
H
I

CREEEEEAK! You open the door to the sleeping quarters carefully. Is someone lurking in the shadows behind the door? All is clear. You spot a sea chest in the corner of the room and go toward it.

13

Which carved column matches this series of carvings?

14

You reach the treasure chest. But which key will fit the lock?

The chest is empty. You will have to continue your search.

15 You are being watched! How many pairs of eyes can you see in this picture?

T **10** S **6** U **12**

You reach the crew's quarters and in the dim light, you trip over something heavy. Cannon balls are lying everywhere!

16

Which pile of cannon balls isn't an odd number?

You move across the crew's quarters toward an opening leading to the next room. Before you can continue, you must solve two more puzzles!

17

Which one of these carvings matches the carving on the cannons?

C

D

A

B

18

There are several stools lying around. Which one is different from the others?

You find yourself in the bilges. **SQUEEEEAL!** There are rats scurrying around at your feet! They appear to be following a scent.

21

How many rats can you see in the picture?

N O P
2 4 6

19

You find four boat hooks. Including the rod, mark the length of each on a piece of paper to find out which is the longest.

20 Which one of these coins does not appear in the picture?

A D B E C

The escape boat is lying on the deck untouched! You go toward it. Complete the last two puzzles and you can collect the clues you need to solve the mysterious message. You are very close to finding the treasure!

22 Can you find the missing piece of rope?

B   A   C   D

23 Look at the carved circles on the boat. If each circle is repeated on the other side of the boat, how many circles are there altogether?

R **10**   S **30**   **20** T

Look again at the scroll you found in the bottle. The symbols represent the puzzles you have solved and the dashes below show the puzzle numbers. If your answers are written down in this order you will see where the treasure can be found!

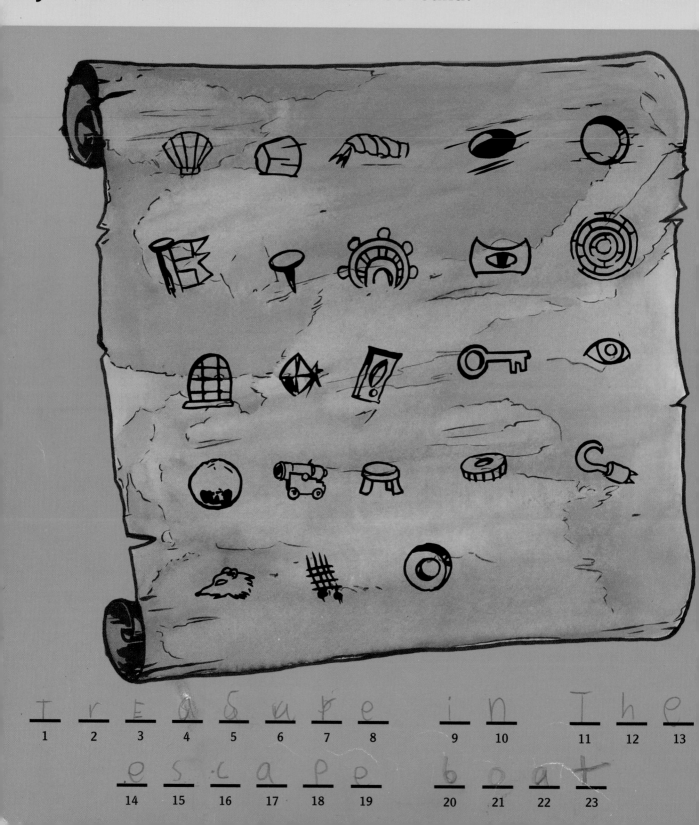

T r e a s u r e   i n   t h e
1 2 3 4 5 6 7 8   9 10   11 12 13

e s c a p e   b o a t
14 15 16 17 18 19   20 21 22 23